Supper Time!

by Damian Harvey and Emma Latham

W
FRANKLIN WATTS
LONDON•SYDNEY

Wolf looked at the clock.

"It's supper time," he said,

licking his lips.

Wolf looked in the cupboard,

but there was nothing to eat.

"Not even a crumb," he said.

Then, Wolf looked through the window.

"Yum!" he said, licking his lips again.

Wolf looked down the hill
at the farmer feeding his chickens.
"A nice juicy chicken," said Wolf.
"That's what I want for supper."

The farmer saw Wolf creeping
down the hill.

"I can see you," yelled the farmer.

"Stay away from my hen house."

Wolf didn't want the farmer
to catch him so he hid in the grass
and waited.
After a while, Little Hen came along.

"Would you like to come to my house for supper?" said Wolf.

"What will we have to eat?" asked Little Hen.

"It's a surprise," smiled Wolf.

"Then I will come," said Little Hen.

Wolf ran up the hill to his house
and waited for Little Hen to come
for supper.

Soon, there was a knock on the door.

"Come in, Little Hen," said Wolf.

"It's supper time."

"Now will you tell me what we're having to eat?" asked Little Hen.

"A nice juicy chicken," Wolf said, licking his lips.

"Oh dear!" said Little Hen.

Little Hen did not run away.
"How are you going to cook
the chicken?" she asked.
"I don't want to cook the chicken,"
said Wolf. "I just want to eat it."

"But it will taste even better
when it's cooked," said Little Hen.
"I can help you."
Wolf licked his lips. He wanted
the chicken to taste even better.
"Yes, please," he said.

"When we have cooked the chicken, we can make a chicken sandwich," said Little Hen. "Let me go out and get some bread."

"I don't like sandwiches," said Wolf. "I just want chicken."

"So we need to light the fire,"
said Little Hen.
Wolf lit the fire and Little Hen put on
some wood.
"The water must be very hot," she said.

Smoke filled the room.

"Let me open the door," said Little Hen.

But again Wolf stopped her.

"We can open the window," said Wolf.

"That's better," he said.

"Oh dear!" said Little Hen.

Soon, the water started to bubble.

"That looks very hot," said Little Hen.

"Is it time to cook the chicken?"

asked Wolf.

"Not yet," said Little Hen.

"We need salt and pepper."

Wolf went to fetch the salt and pepper.

He put some salt into the water.

Little Hen grabbed the pepper pot

and shook it as hard as she could.

Little Hen sneezed and sneezed.
She sneezed so hard that she fell over.
Wolf sneezed too. He sneezed so hard
that he blew the door off.
Little Hen jumped up and ran
as fast as she could.

Wolf turned to chase after her

but then he saw something on the floor.

He licked his lips.

"Yum!" he said. "Supper time!"

Story order

Look at these 5 pictures and captions.
Put the pictures in the right order
to retell the story.

1

Wolf invited Little Hen for supper.

2

Little Hen shook the pepper pot.

Wolf looked at the chickens.

Little Hen laid an egg and ran away.

Wolf wanted to eat Little Hen.

Guide for Independent Reading

This series is designed to provide an opportunity for your child to read on their own. These notes are written for you to help your child choose a book and to read it independently.

In school, your child's teacher will often be using reading books which have been banded to support the process of learning to read. Use the book band colour your child is reading in school to help you make a good choice. *Supper Time!* is a good choice for children reading at Turquoise Band in their classroom to read independently.

The aim of independent reading is to read this book with ease, so that your child enjoys the story and relates it to their own experiences.

About the book

Wolf wants to eat Little Hen for supper so he invites her to his house. But Little Hen is determined to get away!

Before reading

Help your child to learn how to make good choices by asking:
"Why did you choose this book? Why do you think you will enjoy it?"
Look at the cover together and ask: "What do you think the story will be about?" Ask your child to think of what they already know about the story context. Then ask your child to read the title aloud.
Ask: "What do you think Wolf wants to eat for supper?"
Remind your child that they can sound out a word in syllable chunks if they get stuck.
Decide together whether your child will read the story independently or read it aloud to you.

During reading

Remind your child of what they know and what they can do independently. If reading aloud, support your child if they hesitate or ask for help by telling the word. If reading to themselves, remind your child that they can come and ask for your help if stuck.

After reading

Support comprehension by asking your child to tell you about the story. Use the story order puzzle to encourage your child to retell the story in the right sequence, in their own words. The correct sequence can be found on the next page.

Help your child think about the messages in the book that go beyond the story and ask: "Why do you think Little Hen told Wolf she would help him to cook the chicken?"

Give your child a chance to respond to the story: "Did you have a favourite part? What did you think of the ending of the story?"

Extending learning

Help your child understand the story structure by using the same sentence patterning and adding different elements. "Let's make up a new story about Wolf getting his supper. What other animal might Wolf invite over to his house? How might this animal trick Wolf and get away?"

In the classroom, your child's teacher may be teaching about recognising punctuation marks. Ask your child to identify some question marks and exclamation marks in the story and then ask them to practise reading the whole sentences with appropriate expression.

Franklin Watts
First published in Great Britain in 2020
by The Watts Publishing Group

Series Editors: Jackie Hamley and Melanie Palmer
Series Advisors: Dr Sue Bodman and Glen Franklin
Series Designers: Peter Scoulding and Cathryn Gilbert

A CIP catalogue record for this book is
available from the British Library.

ISBN 978 1 4451 7155 5 (hbk)
ISBN 978 1 4451 7156 2 (pbk)
ISBN 978 1 4451 7157 9 (library ebook)

Printed in China

Franklin Watts
An imprint of
Hachette Children's Group
Part of The Watts Publishing Group
Carmelite House
50 Victoria Embankment
London EC4Y 0DZ

An Hachette UK Company
www.hachette.co.uk

www.reading-champion.co.uk

Answer to Story order: 3, 1, 5, 2, 4